STAR OF THE PARTY

A NIGHT SHIFT WITCH MYSTERY

CATE LAWLEY

ALSO BY CATE LAWLEY

VEGAN VAMP MYSTERIES

Adventures of a Vegan Vamp

The Client's Conundrum

The Elvis Enigma

The Nefarious Necklace

The Halloween Haunting

The Selection Shenanigans

The Cupid Caper

The Reluctant Renfield

NIGHT SHIFT WITCH MYSTERIES

Night Shift Witch

Star of the Party

Tickle the Dragon's Tail

Twinkles Takes a Holiday

DEATH RETIRED

Death Retires

A Date with Death

On the Street Where Death Lives

With a Little Bit of Death

FAIRMONT FINDS CANINE COZY MYSTERIES

On the Trail of a Killer

The Scent of a Poet's Past

Sniffing Out Sweet Secrets

Tracking a Poison Pen

CURSED CANDY MYSTERIES

Cutthroat Cupcakes

Twisted Treats

Fatal Fudge

Tea with a Demon: A Cursed Candy Short

Brunch with a Scurry of Squirrels: A Cursed Candy Short

FURRY FAIRY HOLIDAY HIJINKS

Cursed Candy World Mysteries

Candy Cane Conspiracy

Sugar Plum Ploy

Mistletoe Machinations

LOVE EVER AFTER

Heartache in Heels

Skeptic in a Skirt

Pretty in Peep-Toes

Love Ever After Boxed Set One

LUCKY MAGIC

Lucky Magic

Luck of the Devil

Luck of the Draw

Wicked Bad Luck

For the most current listing of Cate's books, visit her website:

www.CateLawley.com

NAUGHTY NUN, FEMME FATALE, WICKED KITTY, OR...SEXY WITCH?

ustin, Texas 1999

WHAT DID a modern woman wear to a Halloween party when she wanted to look sexy but also like she wasn't trying too hard?

I was overthinking this.

It was just a date.

A second date. With my boss. Who I really liked.

Right, I was *not* overthinking. My costume would send a message, whether Ben would consciously notice or not. Also, I wanted to look nice for my date. It would give me confidence.

The naughty nun costume my mentor, Camille,

had lent me was too obvious. I didn't need *that* kind of confidence, the overblown, outrageous kind. Nuns weren't inherently sexy, so I couldn't really be casually glamorous and subtly hot in a slinky nun's outfit.

So, not a nun. I set that costume to the side.

The femme fatale look wasn't any better. The whole point of the costume was to be dangerous and sexy. Nothing understated about that. That costume went into the no pile.

Wicked kitty... That was a possibility. Then again, cats and I weren't especially fond of one another. One fluffy gray cat in particular came to mind. Twinkles and I barely coexisted. We certainly weren't friendly.

And now that I was thinking of Twinkles, there was no way that I could possibly wear the wicked kitty costume.

I opened the last garment bag. This contribution was from my mom's closet, so I wasn't holding out much hope.

But as soon as I slid the zipper down and saw the silver and black beads and then the spangles at the hemline, I knew this was the winner.

My mother was one of those women who'd managed to pop out a kid and then return to her pre-baby weight *and then* kept it off for basically ever. I could only hope I got those genes and not my dad's side of the family. They all seemed to have slid into middle age in the normal way, slowly gaining weight with each passing decade.

Long story short, my mom and I were the same dress size. Not a fact I'd ever thought would come in handy, since she tended to favor beige khakis, appliqued shirts, and Keds.

I slipped the dress on, mostly because I figured there was a catch. Sometimes a plain dress on the rack became slinky and sexy when worn, so the opposite might also be true. Probably was true. My mother wasn't exactly the sexy siren type.

But no. It couldn't have been more perfect.

The dress's hem ended midthigh, though the spangles hanging down from the hem gave the illusion of covering more leg. The neckline wasn't particularly daring, but it didn't need to be because the dress hugged my curves, and the beading shouted, "Check out my assets."

Yeah, my mom and I were having a chat about where the heck she'd worn this costume.

Only after I'd taken it off did I find the price tag.

Good news for me, because if I was getting lucky in this dress, I really didn't want to consider the possibility that my mother had used it for the same purpose. Ick.

Decision made, I turned my attention to accessories.

And also to the wisdom of inviting my boss, who

happened to be fully human without an ounce of magic, to a Halloween party thrown by a bunch of witches.

Maybe this hadn't been such a great idea for a second date.

But I'd already RSVP'd for two and told Camille that I was planning to bring Ben.

Camille adored Ben, so she'd never let me hear the end of it if I chickened out at the last minute.

That problem solved—or put on hold—I moved on to the weighty matter of shoes.

What sort of shoes did a girl wear with a flapper dress?

DARING SECOND DATES

Ben picked me up right on time.

Of course he did. Ben was like that. He was reliable, considerate, and generally a stand-up guy. Being consistently punctual was his way of telling me he respected my time, and I adored that about him.

Ben couldn't be more different from the men I'd dated before. First, he was a *man*.

My dating history was peppered with bad boys. The kind who were exciting and fun...

Until they stuck you with the check, even though they knew you had no cash.

Until they showed up late, even though you were relying on them for a ride and had to wait in what wasn't the safest part of town.

Until they slept with your neighbor, because:

"What? You thought we were exclusive? Come on, babe. I never said that."

My bad boys had suffered from a complete absence of goals, a tendency to mooch, unpredictable moods, and a lack of fidelity.

Until Alex, my last boyfriend.

Maybe Alex had been my transition guy. The one I'd actually loved, but who hadn't been right for me, because... So many reasons. I loved him like a dear friend, but I wasn't *in love* with him. Thank goodness. Ben deserved more than rebound status.

Alex was the first man I'd dated who respected me, pushed me to do more, challenged me to be better.

He was just as moody as the rest of my bad boys, but Alex's darkness came from lived experiences. He was no spoiled brat, no selfish man-child. Alex needed someone to bring light into his life, and I hadn't been that person.

The age gap had also been a problem. Alex was older than toilet paper, and that had impacted our relationship in ways I hadn't expected. I didn't need a replacement dad. Or even an overprotective, hovering boyfriend. No thank you.

But I had to wonder if dating Alex with all his moody care and brooding consideration hadn't given me a glimpse of what it would be like to date a nice guy.

And then I'd met Ben.

A guy who took over his family's business when he was much too young, because it was the right thing to do. A guy who spent his working hours skillfully and compassionately interacting with grief-stricken clients. A guy who treated me like I was special. Like I deserved his time, limited though it was.

When I opened the door, his eyes widened, and then a smile spread across his face. Ben was a handsome guy, but Ben with an appreciative gleam in his eyes? Smoking hot.

"You look gorgeous." He leaned closer and kissed my cheek, careful of the bold red lipstick I'd applied.

"Thank you," I replied. Accepting compliments had been difficult initially. The bad boys hadn't given many, and while Alex had been appreciative, he was also a reticent guy in general. "Love the gangster casual look."

I'd told Ben I was going with a twenties look, but also not to make too much of a fuss over his costume.

He'd opted for a pair of dress slacks, a dress shirt with the sleeves rolled up, and a pair of nicely shined shoes—all items he wore on a daily basis at work. But he'd added a wide tie and a vest that could pass for period attire. Add in his fedora, put him next to me (where he would be the entirety of the night, given the nature of the party), and his costume more than passed muster.

Also, his vest hugged his muscular chest in a *very* nice way.

It was too tempting to resist. I patted his firm chest. "Love the vest."

He chuckled, because he knew exactly what I really loved. "Glad to hear it. Anything I should know about this party? Other than it's hosted by a bunch of witches?"

"Stay close, don't eat or drink anything I haven't tried first, and avoid anything that might be a familiar."

The look on his face. Priceless.

"I'm kidding, Ben. You can eat the appetizers. You can even guzzle the champagne, if you don't mind me driving us home."

He chuckled. "Should have known when you mentioned familiars."

Ben was well aware of my contentious relationship with Twinkles, Camille's cat. As a result of various conversations concerning the fiendish feline, he also knew that familiars weren't a reality in witchy life. Witches had a complicated relationship with their pets, but we didn't have familiars.

"You ready for this?"

He grinned. "Absolutely."

And it truly seemed like he was.

He wanted a glimpse of my witchy life, because it was a part of me. And I'd wanted to feel like I could include him in all aspects of my life without worrying he'd freak out when he stumbled on something not quite human.

It might only be our second official date, but Ben and I spent a lot of time together. That happened when you dated the boss. We were well beyond second-date level in most parts of our relationship.

And sure, a Halloween party hosted by a bunch of witches was maybe a more immersive experience when it came to magical exposure than I could have chosen, but it was nothing compared to my first few days working at the funeral home. A murdered golem. Working with my wizard ex. Getting the all clear to keep his memory from the magical community's version of a sheriff.

If he could handle all of *that* and still want to go out with me, Ben was a trouper. One little witch-filled shindig wouldn't be a problem.

Right?

And for a while, everything *was* all right.

We drove to the freaky house on the hill that totally looked like a haunted mansion from a horror flick. Ben didn't make the comparison, just said it was a gorgeous home. Also true, but the horror vibes were definitely there, aided by the early onset of night and a full moon.

Ben and Camille hugged like old friends. I guess baking a body together had bonded them.

Then Ben met a few more witches.

Then we decided to "explore the house."

Maybe sneaking away to a remote part of the creepy horror house for a kiss—or two—hadn't been the best idea.

Then again, who would have thought we'd find a body?

That was definitely when the date took a turn for the worse.

3

CORPUS INTERRUPTUS

A dead flapper.

Just my luck, the body had to be decked out in 1920s' finery.

As I eyed the dead woman Ben and I had just discovered sprawled across the master bathtub, I lost some of my enthusiasm for the sexy beaded and spangled number I was sporting. Looked like this costume wasn't getting a repeat. Finding a dead woman wearing similar attire had pretty much killed the fun of it.

Thanks for that, Isabella.

Naturally, I knew the dead woman; I knew all the witches at the party.

Isabella Treece was a powerhouse witch from a neighboring city. She'd come to celebrate with her dear friend Margery, the owner of the house and one of the party's hosts.

Margery was going to flip.

I swallowed a groan and leaned closer to inspect the body. She was draped over the edge of the large tub, her vacant stare aimed just above my left shoulder.

"Wait, Star, don't." Ben held out his arm, just like a mom who'd slammed on the brakes. It was protective in a way that would be kind of cute but for the corpse.

Wet strands of blonde hair clung to Isabella's face and neck. Her mascara had run and her lipstick was smudged. And she was utterly still, a stillness only the dead can achieve. And I was expert now that I'd worked in a funeral home for several weeks.

I grasped Ben's hand, gently squeezed his fingers, then moved his arm. Not that I planned to touch Isabella—not with the cloud of dark magic surrounding her. Ducking my head close to his, I whispered, "She's a witch. Someone's drowned her."

Drowning with a dollop of dark magic: it was an excellent way to kill a witch.

Something about being immersed in water prevented self-healing. I was trying to remember the mechanics—it really was something I should know —when an ear-piercing shriek interrupted my train of thought.

A human. It had to be.

I swallowed a sigh. No way Ben and I were keeping this quiet now.

I turned to find Camille, my mentor and also one of the designated hosts of the party, intercepting a guest at the bathroom door. Definitely a human.

Camille moved to block the doorway. "Best not to touch anything."

The woman looked dismayed. "I'm a doctor. I can help…" But then she closed her eyes and tilted her head. When she opened them, she said, "You're right, of course. She's past reviving. And we shouldn't touch anything before the police arrive."

As she spoke, several more guests gathered behind her and Camille, including Margery, the owner of the house.

At the mention of police, Margery snapped her fingers.

With an electric pop, magic filled the air. Since this was her home, I'd guess she had some sort of security system in place that she'd just activated.

She slipped by both the doctor and Camille and did her best to block the view of the partygoers.

For just a moment—a very brief moment—I could see her grief. Nothing like tears. I couldn't even imagine Margery crying. Just a terrible sadness.

Then it was wiped away as if it had never been, and she turned to me with a hard look.

Her inspection lasted several long seconds, then she turned to Ben.

Just wonderful. We'd found the body, so we'd become immediate suspects.

Which was ridiculous. Of any of the witches at the party, I was the least likely to commit violence against Isabella. I didn't know her nearly as well as the other witches present, and it was widely known that I was a strong proponent of tightening up the witch community's sad excuse for a justice system.

Her silent appraisal was interrupted by one of the guests calling out, "My mobile phone doesn't have a signal."

A human, because only a human would be surprised.

Who had thought it was a good idea to invite humans to this bash?

Ben shifted, reminding me that I'd brought my own human guest. Ben was different, but he was still fully human without a jot of magic.

"Anyone have a signal?" The same human, a young woman from the sound of her voice.

A few quietly murmured "no" replies followed, so Margery's house was either in a mobile phone black hole and no one had noticed until now, or a more likely scenario, she'd shut down the signal. That particular skill wasn't in my repertoire, but I'd bet it wasn't difficult with a little prep.

Margery didn't seem to be in any hurry to manage the witnesses, so I glanced hopefully at Ben.

He squeezed my shoulder, then turned to the group. "Why don't we all step back? I'm sure the...ah, the police will want the scene preserved."

Since Margery and Camille were now both busy studying the corpse and ignoring the guests, it was a good thing he was taking charge. Having a funeral director on hand in a crisis—a funeral director who accepted a reality wherein the police would *not* be called—was handy.

Margery rose from her position next to the body. "The kitchen, Mr. Kawolski, if you would be so kind. That's the best place for everyone to gather. I'm sure Star can manage without you for a few minutes."

While I'd teased him about not eating or drinking anything until I'd tried it, I'd told him in all seriousness on the car ride over to stick close to me. So I gave him a subtle head nod to let him know he should follow Margery's directive.

Once reassured, Ben herded everyone out of the master bedroom and into the hall.

A few seconds later, only two stragglers remained, Grayson and Samantha, both witches, both dressed in pirate garb. Samantha gave me a nasty look as I joined them in the master bedroom. "Was that your human?"

I opened my mouth—but Camille cut me off.

"This isn't the time for politics, Samantha, not unless you think a human guest could have managed this?" Camille waited with an expectant expression.

"Don't be foolish. No human is capable of this." Margery waved a hand in the direction of Isabella's body. "Magic is involved."

Samantha's nostrils flared and her jaw clenched, but she didn't say a word.

Except for Ben, none of the humans present knew witches existed—at least not in an official capacity—so even excluding the use of magic, it was a ridiculous stretch to think a human was involved.

The master bath was roomy, in keeping with the well-over-four-thousand-square-foot house, but with five witches in the space it seemed a lot smaller, and I was starting to feel antsy. Which then prompted what should have been an obvious question. Why would more than one person even be in the bathroom? I didn't know Isabella very well, but it did seem a little odd.

"Who would Isabella have been in the bathroom with?" I directed the question to Margery, since they were close friends.

Margery turned her attention to Grayson. "Well?"

"How would I know?" He adjusted the sword at his hip, a defensive gesture if ever I saw one. "She's not my mentor any longer. Hasn't been for over a week now."

Margery shot him a sharp look, and his hand dropped to his side.

I rolled my eyes. As if Grayson the witch trainee was about to draw a weapon on Margery.

Samantha glanced at the door. She looked like she was regretting her choice to stay.

Margery flicked a hand, and the door closed with a decisive snick. "Perhaps, but since you two were especially close, I thought you might know." She paused. "It wasn't me."

The implication, of course, being that it was Grayson. But I was having a hard time seeing him scrounge up enough backbone to actually kill a witch.

Tight-lipped, but with a reasonably respectful tone, Grayson said, "It wasn't me either."

"You." Margery pointed at me. "You discovered the body. What were you doing in this part of the house?"

"And with that human," Samantha said, giving me a sickly sweet smile.

"Ah...we were..." How did one say "looking for a dark, secluded corner" while still maintaining the respect of one's human-hating witch colleagues? Sticky.

Luckily, the sound of shattering glass saved me.

4

___

A MURKY COSMIC MESSAGE

Mirror glass covered a good third of the tiled bathroom floor, but as I looked around at the occupants, no one was visibly injured.

"What in the world?" Samantha said.

What else could it be but a ghost? That, or one of the witches I was crammed into the bathroom with had been hiding hardcore telekinetic expertise. Shattering a mirror took some force, and therefore some decent telekinetic talent.

My gaze locked with Camille's. If her expression was anything to go by, she was thinking the same thing.

"Spit it out then," Margery barked. She wagged a finger at Camille and then me. "I can see the wheels turning."

"It's too soon for Isabella to manifest from another plane—if she even will—so unless you've got a haunting here in the house..." Camille shrugged delicately.

"Perhaps. Unless someone wants to fess up to shattering the mirror?" Margery leveled each of the witches in the bathroom—myself included—with a penetrating stare. I could feel the push of magic as her gaze met mine.

"You know none of us is capable," Samantha said. "Which means it has to be a ghost. But how could that be? It's not like you'd host a party if your house was harboring a specter."

Margery straightened her spine. "If that's your less-than-subtle way of criticizing my abilities, I can tell you that I suspected. I've done a few cleansings, but the presence persists. I invited Isabella with an eye to addressing any potential otherworldly problems."

"But..." Camille's eyed widened. "But Isabella arrived after the party had begun. You did *not* host a party in a potentially haunted house. Margery!"

Lips thin, Margery said, "She was late. And I... Well, it's not important." She scanned the bathroom, but must not have picked up anything out of the ordinary, because she turned back to us with an annoyed look. "And it might not even be a typical haunting. What ghost moves into a house already inhabited by a witch?"

"Margery." Grayson's gaze had locked on to Isabella's lifeless form. He looked concerned—not so unusual, since she'd been his mentor, but...something was off. Had he noticed something we'd all missed?

"What, Grayson?" Margery snapped. "Spit it out."

Expression blank, he said, "Her veil's missing."

"A veil? With a flapper costume?" I couldn't see how that fit, and the rest of her costume was flawless. Even the shoes looked vintage twenties era.

"No, he's right." Without the attitude Samantha had been flinging around all night, she said, "She used it as a headscarf, tied to the side."

A helpful Samantha stood out as highly suspect, but that could just be nerves speaking.

I was feeling a little paranoid about sharing such a small space with a murder victim. Also, possibly, the murderer. If I thought about it too much, my head would start to spin, so I turned my attention back to the present.

Camille clasped her hands. She wasn't the type, but if she had been, I'd say she was wringing them. "Oh my, it's *that* veil, isn't it?"

"All right, I'll bite," I said. "What's with the scarf?"

"Veil," Grayson corrected me.

"Okay, veil," I said. "What's with the veil?"

"It belonged to one of the Fox family," Margery said. When recognition didn't immediately spark in my eyes, she turned a stern look on Camille. "Have you taught her nothing? Our history can't be ignored, even the unsavory parts."

The unsavory parts were the good bits, and I *didn't* ignore those, but I also had no clue what they were talking about. Camille was my mentor, and I didn't want her to get any more flack for my less-than-studious habits, so I refrained from comment and hoped someone would elaborate.

Samantha made a disgusted noise. "Everyone knows about the Foxes and their claims of communication with the other side, even the mundane world. But the real witch in the family was a little-known cousin."

Grayson's lip curled. "That's the one. It was her veil."

A witch family that could not only see but also communicate with ghosts, an attribute normally found in wizard families, and not the particularly reputable ones. How downright shameful for a respectable witch family.

Hard eye roll. Witch families could be so snobby. I was happy to be the only one in mine.

As for the veil and what that had to do with the

Fox cousin, it was a known phenomenon that especially talented individuals could imbue objects with some of their magical skills. My guess was that long-lost cousin had been in deep mourning and worn the veil frequently. Possibly she'd died while wearing it, or it had been a favorite item, but however it had happened, that veil ended up with some magical mojo. And it was here, in this house.

Since cleansing a house of ghosts—basically chasing them away—didn't require communication, and communicating with ghosts was frowned upon, why had Isabella brought the veil?

Margery had already been cagey about the haunting, but it had to be asked.

"Why not just cleanse the house?" I asked Margery. "Why have Isabella reach out?"

Samantha and Grayson turned to Margery with expectant expressions.

Margery gave me a narrow-eyed look, but the pirate duo's interest must have exerted just enough pressure, because she finally replied, "I wanted to know if there might be some significance to the haunting. *If* there's a haunting. I've cleansed the house several times now, and it just keeps coming back. Whatever it is, whoever it is, they're a nuisance. Twelve times it's bounced back here —twelve!"

"And the party was a good time to have that chat?" Camille asked incredulously. "Without mentioning it to me, your cohost?"

Margery's expression turned mulish. "Well, she was late, wasn't she? It should have all been taken care of long before you arrived."

Samantha tipped her head, looking at Margery with more than a little interest. "It is especially odd that he or she keeps returning, isn't it? Being cleansed from a space can't be particularly pleasant for a ghost. Why here? Why *your* house?"

"If I knew that, I wouldn't have needed Isabella and the veil," Margery snapped. A split second later, she said, "And it's not as if communication with the otherworld is strictly forbidden. It's not against the law or anything."

She seemed awfully defensive for a woman completely in the dark. My witch antennae, if there were such a thing, were telling me she knew something about her visitor. "Who do you—"

"Enough," Margery interrupted with a glance in my direction. "Annalise probably put the whole lot of humans to sleep, but that can't last forever. It's past time we take a closer look at the body."

As everyone else turned to Isabella, I scanned first the bathroom, then my probable list of suspects: Margery, Samantha, and Grayson. Camille wasn't involved. That I knew in my heart. And if I was proven wrong, it was time to move to the middle of nowhere and live in complete isolation, because that meant that no one was trustworthy.

CeeCee and Bernard, also witches, were in the kitchen with Ben and the other guests and likely doing their best to keep Annalise in check. None of the three of them were in the clear but were much further down the list of suspects. Outside of being generally good people, they'd surely want in on the investigation and would have stayed close if either was guilty.

Annalise... She was an enigma. She was a witch with an itchy trigger finger, and from Margery's comment, in possession of a well-known knockout spell. Perhaps how Isabella had been overpowered? Though not a fan of humans, there was something vulnerable and innocent about Annalise. I couldn't see her as the killer, but I had to assume it wasn't impossible.

The only people I could cross off the list were Camille and the humans, including Ben.

Margery was a pretty good suspect. She was acting more than a little suspicious and was obviously withholding information about the haunting. Samantha and Grayson were generally shady characters, so it wouldn't shock me if either of them had done the deed. Grayson even had a recent history with Isabella.

I sighed. I loved being a witch, but our community had problems. Serious, deeply ingrained, legal, ethical, and judicial problems.

As I turned my attention to the body, I couldn't help but wonder if the cosmos was trying to send me a message. I'd recently nabbed a second job at a funeral home, immediately discovered a murdered golem, and now I'd stumbled on my second murder victim. All within a few weeks.

If the universe was speaking to me, it wasn't sending a particularly pleasant message.

Camille nudged me and whispered, "Star, watch out."

Grayson and Samantha were lifting Isabella's damp form and laying her out on the floor. I had to sidestep to keep the dripping water off my shoes.

"We're not calling emergency response?" I tried for a nonchalant tone, but Margery's sharp look made it clear I'd failed on that count.

"I'll consider calling Cornelius and his thugs just as soon as he hires his first witch responder." Margery knelt next to Isabella. "This is a witch problem, and witches will handle it. No calling that boyfriend of yours."

I didn't have a boyfriend. Ben and I were on our second date, but then, that wasn't who Margery meant. She was referring to my *ex*. Alex led Cornelius's emergency response team.

I didn't correct her. What was the point? She'd met my date. But her refusal made me inwardly cringe.

Knowing I was risking the wrath of Margery, I said, "Technically, we're all suspects."

"Suspects of what?" Since Margery was examining the murdered woman, that seemed a laughable statement. "This is hardly a crime. It's a private witch matter. One that we'll handle amongst ourselves."

The Society for the Study of Paranormal and Occult Phenomena, the closest thing to a government that we had, wasn't likely to argue. Especially if Isabella's death was presented to them nicely wrapped up in a tidy package of lies and influence.

Cornelius, the Society's chief security officer, talked a good game. He *said* he wanted to move the Society into the current century, hence emergency response's new name. They used to just be called enforcers.

But modernization was sticky. The Society was comprised of a group of people, all longer-lived than humans, who were both stuck in the past and possessed enhancements that gave them some amount of power over mortal mundanes.

"We could make her body disappear." Grayson

met my startled gaze and shrugged. "What? She's dead. We can't change that. And you're not wrong when you say we're suspects. Cornelius has been onto emergency response about actually investigating the deaths of important Society members. If she disappears, this all just goes away."

And that wasn't a suspicious comment. Not at all. I nudged him a little higher up the suspect list.

Samantha pursed her lips disapprovingly. "She was *your* mentor. How—"

"Ex-mentor," Grayson corrected. "And are you telling me you *wouldn't* like all this to disappear?"

Samantha didn't respond.

Camille had been picking up shards of glass while Samantha and Grayson bickered. She chucked the last few pieces into the bin, then cleared her throat. She addressed the room with a quiet authority I only rarely saw her demonstrate.

"Margery is right. Emergency response are only a step away from the thugs they've always been. We do need to handle this ourselves." She held up a hand when Margery started to reply. "But Star's right. Everyone here with an ounce of magic is suspect."

Camille might not have the mega witch wattage that Margery did, but she was an effective, reliable witch. She was respected and had pull in the community. If she wasn't satisfied with the results we came up with and brought Isabella's death to the attention of the Society, it wouldn't be ignored.

Way to go, Camille.

My impromptu investigation had just gained legs and turned semiofficial.

5

A HALLOWEEN HICCUP

A soft knock broke the silence that followed Camille's pronouncement.

Ben stood in the open doorway of the bathroom. "Does that mean all the non-magical attendees can leave when they wake up? Sorry to interrupt, it's just that one of the witches has knocked them all out."

"You are most certainly not excused," Margery said forcefully. "We have to assure that non-magical attendees leave with the appropriate memories, none of which should include a dead person."

Ben shared a look with me, and I wanted to hug him. A surprising response, but he looked so completely unruffled, by Margery, by the dead body, by the magical nonsense that was clearly afoot.

He'd mastered a mix of courtesy and helpfulness with a dash of deference that I'd seen him use on his most difficult clients, and that was the tone he adopted now. "I understand, but couldn't we tell them it's a murder-mystery party? From Annalise's description, they should wake up somewhat disoriented and suggestible."

Margery considered his suggestion, but it was Camille who quickly agreed with a smile of thanks. "It's a fabulous idea. It's win-win—isn't that what you people say?"

By "you people," I figured she meant anyone born after Woodstock, otherwise known as "young people."

Margery put her hands on her hips. "I suppose someone needs to check on everyone camped in the kitchen." Her brow furrowed as I lifted my hand. "Yes, you would like to put your nose in it, wouldn't you?" With a curt nod, she said, "Off you go, then. And don't expect any help from Camille sorting them out. She'll be busy helping me with the examination."

I nodded, hooked an arm in Ben's, and exited at a good clip before she could sic Samantha or Grayson on us. I had a few goals in mind, none of which would be furthered by the pirate duo tagging along.

First things first: check on the humans and make

sure Annalise hadn't been too enthusiastic with her knockout spell. "Kitchen first."

"Yes." Ben gave me a funny look. "That is the plan."

"I also need to keep an eye out for a ghost. Long story short, the house might be haunted and the ghost might be the murderer, though it would be hard for a noncorporeal entity to drown a witch, and I'm not very good at detecting them—" I took a breath and exhaled. "Sorry."

He reached for my hand and gently pulled me to a stop. We were halfway to the kitchen, just at the top of the stairs leading to the main entryway.

"You're allowed to be a little flustered. Murder can do that." Then he leaned down and kissed me.

A few very pleasant seconds later, he leaned back and said, "Since we were interrupted earlier and I don't see a murder investigation lending itself to a lot of 'us' time." When my shoulders relaxed a few inches, he said, "Better. We'll get this sorted out."

"I'm just bummed that *this* is our second date."

He twined his fingers with mine. "No problem. I enjoy spending time with you, even if I have to do it during a murder investigation. And I'm sure you'll figure it out." He kissed me again, then said, "Better?"

I nodded. "Uh-huh." Then, as his words sank in, I said, much more firmly, "I'm sure that we will. Now

I just have to figure out how to spot a ghost, not something witches are particularly skilled at—even the good ones."

"You're the best, so I have faith."

I wasn't the best—I didn't study enough to be—but I wasn't terrible. I had to give it a try either way. And, heck, if I was lucky and the apparition was close and interacting on this plane, I might even pick up a trace of suspicious magic. I wouldn't be able to see it, of course, unless...

"For Pete's sake," I muttered.

"What now?"

"Sorry, I just realized it's Halloween."

"Star, we're at a Halloween party. It's definitely Halloween, but what does that have to do with anything?"

"Other than I'm an idiot for missing the obvious, it means there's at least a chance that our ghost is walking around corporeally right now."

"Whoa, they can do that?" But then he shook his head and with a bemused expression said, "Why not? There are people walking around that were created using corpses as parts. I guess a flesh-and-blood ghost isn't that far afield."

"To be fair, golems are a weird concept even for witches. But, to the point, if there's a ghost and all the requirements for corporeal manifestation have been met, then it's even more likely that the he or she is involved in the murder."

And that was when I felt someone shove my shoulder hard. As I lost my balance, my panicky gaze fixated on the two flights of hardwood stairs I was about to tumble down.

6

MY HERO

My shoulder wrenched uncomfortably as Ben yanked me from the precipice and dragged me several feet back from the stairs.

As he hugged me against his chest, I couldn't help a small—probably mildly hysterical—giggle. Thank goodness for Ben's fast reflexes. Who knew he could move so quickly?

Ben peered down at me and said, "Are you okay?" My normally unflappable boss was breathing hard. My near tumble had stolen his breath.

"Uh-huh." After our last murder-mystery adventure, I'd been taking the time to work on my healing skills. And while I still wasn't fabulous at on-the-fly healing, I thought I might have perfected a catch-all potion. I pulled out a small vial from the tiny clutch

I'd paired with my flapper costume. "Magic healing in a pill."

I popped one and then used a little of my magic and a lot of intent to focus the pill for best effect.

Magic in the moment versus prepared magic had become a question worth studying after I'd been caught with my magical pants metaphorically down. There'd been some gunfire, a touch of bluffing, and just enough magic to barely pull Ben and me out of a nasty situation.

Mostly we'd been rescued by my ex, Alex. I liked to think I could rescue myself, but since the facts weren't supporting that fanciful assumption, I'd started taking my studies much more seriously.

Camille had the expertise to do incredible things with prepared potions and spells, and I had—somewhere deep inside me—some serious witch wattage. Why not combine the two to best effect? It just seemed practical. Witches like Margery, witches with greater natural gifts, didn't work that way. In their mind, power—witch wattage—was everything. Then again, Margery had used a prepared security spell... That was an idea to explore more fully later. When there wasn't a corpse waiting to have its murderer revealed.

Feeling a little more like myself, I took stock of the surrounding area. I flipped on my erratic magical sight and found absolutely nothing.

"And?" Ben asked. "You're doing that thing you do, right? Where you look for magic?"

"I am. I'm just not finding anything."

Ben firmly grasped my hand. "How about we head down the stairs, but I don't let go."

I nodded.

Ben knew a tumble down the stairs wasn't likely to do much damage to me unless some magic was involved, but I couldn't blame the guy for being cautious. *I* was worried. Also, it would still hurt like crazy.

"Any chance you know why this ghost is giving you grief?" Ben asked.

"I'm still not a hundred percent it's a ghost. It could be telekinesis."

Ben raised his eyebrows. "So that's a thing. Do all witches have telekinetic powers?"

"No, definitely not, so a ghost seems more likely. Oh, I forgot to tell you." I filled him in on the Fox sister–cousin veil connection as we headed down the stairs—but I also had a death grip on the railing as I descended.

When I'd finished my tale of witch taboos and Margery's shady ghost communication plans, Ben said, "Definitely a ghost. Why does Margery want to talk to this ghost so badly?"

I could hear conversation in the kitchen. Nothing distinct, just the murmuring of voices, but I stopped and lowered my voice. "She claims to figure out why it wouldn't leave on a permanent basis. She claims it's bounced back here twelve times. If it did, that's excessive."

A colorfully dressed raven-haired woman popped her head out from around the corner. "Sexy gypsy" was the look I *thought* she was going for. With Annalise, one never knew for sure.

"I can hear you," she said in a singsong voice. Then in normal tones, she added, "But it's a good thing, because I know all the answers to your questions. Come on, Star, join us in the kitchen. We're having a little party." She smiled flirtatiously at me, then gave Ben a less enthusiastic look. "And you can bring him, too."

"Thanks, Annalise." I was always polite but never too friendly, because she was so hard for me to read.

And our politics didn't align. I actually liked humans.

She quite liked me, but her motivations remained a mystery. I hadn't yet determined if her interest was romantic or in some way tied to my magical potential. Either way, I didn't entirely trust her—and that was before she'd become a murder suspect.

I gave Ben a commiserating look, and we both followed her into the kitchen. As I rounded the corner, a rather surprising sight greeted me: five people, sitting around a large kitchen table, propped in various states of repose. It was as if they'd all been sitting down to tea and then drunk roofied beverages.

"Well, this is an improvement," Ben said. I eyed him askance, and he held up his hands. "Hey, better than sprawled all over the kitchen floor. That's how they were when I left."

"So what exactly are the side effects, Annalise?" I asked.

She inspected her bright red nails and didn't comment.

Bernard said, "Shy all of a sudden, Annalise? Come on now."

"Bernard." I flashed a genuine smile at him. I didn't want to believe he was a suspect. Bernard was like me, from a non-witching family. Witches might be made, not born, but that didn't mean there weren't strong familial ties in the witching community. Magic had found Bernard and I around the same age, and we'd followed the path all the way to full transformation around the same time. I couldn't believe he was involved with a murder.

Bernard stood up from the stool where he'd been perched and stretched. Everyone towered over me, but Bernard was tall by anyone's standards. When he was done, he said, "Little Miss Zappy was chattier earlier, and now that you're here she's suddenly gone quiet."

Bernard was low wattage. He didn't have the juice to make a big splash in the more traditional witching world. And unlike Camille, he didn't have a knack (or the patience) for potions, but Bernard had a way with the written word. Someday he'd make his mark as a spellmaster. He just wasn't quite there yet, and he didn't seem to be in any hurry.

He flashed me a cheeky grin. "How you been, Star?" He glanced at Ben. "Busy?"

I'd say we were similar in our lack of commercial ambition, but I'd recently been kicked in the pants, motivationally speaking, and was probably a little more inclined to study than Bernard. "Yes, busy—but not the way you mean. You've met Ben?"

Before Bernard could do more than give Ben and me a speculative look, CeeCee emerged from the pantry. "Hey, sweetie." She was carrying what looked like a bottle of home-brew beer. "I was just raiding the pantry for anything that might help Annalise's victims with the nasty hangover they're gonna have in an hour or so. I'm working on a quick-brew healing potion that should do the trick. Low potency, but enough to take away the sharpest edge." She gestured to a punch bowl on the butcher's block island. "Wanna check it out? See if it needs anything else?"

CeeCee was quite adept at potions. Unlike Bernard and me, she came from a witching family and had completed her transformation with an eye ever turned toward a profitable future.

"No. I'm sure your odds-and-ends, last-minute brew is better than anything I could cook up. Your potions are nothing short of inspired."

She accepted the compliment without a blush. She knew she was fabulous. I didn't want to think she had anything to do with murder—and the resident ghost *was* looking highly suspect—but...

With a slightly mischievous look, she said, "We're in the clear, Star darling. Bernard and I are an item now, so we've been in each other's pockets all night. And if that heavily biased alibi doesn't suit, Annalise has been trailing close behind for most of the evening."

An odd thing for Annalise to do.

Annalise shrugged. "Bernard just has something..." And then she let loose a facsimile of a wistful sigh.

"Um-hm. Bernard has me, and you always were one for the unattainable, weren't you, darling?" CeeCee set the bottle down with a dull thud on the butcher block.

I wasn't particularly interested in pursuing the more drama-laden aspects of their lives, but if it related to Isabella's death, it had to be done. "Okay, so to be clear, you're all alibiing each other...for the whole evening?"

"We don't have a time of death yet," Ben added.

"Ah, but we do," Annalise said. She looked quite pleased with herself. "Grayson and Isabella had a huge blowup about an hour ago, and since then, we've all been together."

The window had just narrowed—a lot. Isabella had been killed within the last hour, a much firmer timeline than we'd previously had. It wasn't like Isabella had been found with a little sticky note saying "this just happened" on her forehead.

Our first truly helpful clue. And I also needed to rejigger my suspect list. Grayson had just shot to the top.

7

GHOST CRASHER

As I considered my mental list of who-coulda-dunit, I realized that I had three suspects tied for first place: Margery, with her secretive otherworldly communications; the ghost, who had either tried to kill me or was incredibly inept at communicating from the other side; and now Grayson, who'd had a heated argument with Isabella not an hour before she'd been found dead.

At least the people at the party that I actually liked had an alibi. CeeCee and Bernard as killers would have significantly dented the small amount of faith in the witching world I had left.

"Ah, what's with the hangovers?" Ben asked, looking flummoxed. "Can't you create a concoction that knocks them out without the side effects?"

Annalise boosted herself onto the butcher block, then, with her Doc Martens knocking against the wood, said, "It's the memory fizz I added. It leaves a nasty headache. Nothing I can do."

"Memory fizz?" Ben said. His voice was calm—when was he not?—but something was off with his posture.

Ben had come close to having his own memory zapped not so very long ago. And he knew—because I'd told him—that it wasn't always as surgical a procedure as it should be. Depending on who was doing it and what memories were being wiped, it could be a little more like a sledgehammer to the head.

"Memory fizz." Annalise shrugged. "I almost went with 'fizzle' then decided it sounded weird. I short-circuit the part of the memory that's attached to getting knocked out. It usually erases a few minutes before I zapped them, which is handy. It also makes the recipient open to certain ideas that I might plant when they wake up."

"Not helping, Annalise." Bernard ambled over to Ben and held out his hand. "We didn't officially meet earlier. I'm Bernard."

Ben paused for a split second then grasped Bernard's hand and nodded at him.

Bernard said, "Annalise can be dense—"

"Hey!" The thudding of her Doc Martens stopped.

"—but she's not as bad as she sounds. What she's not saying is that her particular method is much safer than the usual memory wipe. And if her combo spell plus raw magic works the way it should, then there's no reason for the Society to wipe their memories later. That process is what causes damage."

"*Can* cause damage," CeeCee said. "It depends on..." She bit her lip when she caught sight of Ben's expression. "I'm really sorry."

Bernard joined CeeCee and put his arm around her shoulders as he sniffed at the concoction she was mixing. "No one thinks you're out to destroy mankind."

Annalise's lips twisted into a kind of sympathetic grimace. "Humans are a pain...but no one needs their brains scrambled like that."

And time to change the subject.

"So..." I eyed the group of snoozing humans, five slumped and apparently slumbering figures. "Everyone here at the table is okay for a while, and minus some confusion when they wake up, we're all good?"

"Yep." Annalise pulled a lollipop out of one of her pockets. She offered it to me and, when I declined, tore off the wrapper and popped the lollipop in her mouth.

CeeCee checked the time. "You've got forty-five minutes at most, so unless you want Annalise zapping them again—"

"I don't mind," Annalise said around the lollipop.

"Let's be clear," CeeCee said, "you don't want Annalise zapping them again. I suspect that the result would be the mother of all migraines."

"Right, Ben and I are on it." I realized belatedly that I hadn't actually asked him if he was on board with hunting down a magical killer. He could just hang out in the kitchen with the eliminated suspects. After how cool he was the last time, I just assumed he'd want in. Surely he would have said... I shot him an inquisitive look.

And I'd swear he winked at me. It was quick, and maybe it was more of a blink—Nope, he winked. If he had some magic, I'd be guessing at some mind-reading abilities about now.

A quick mental tally had the household head count at fourteen when the body had been discovered. I said, "As far as attendees go, we've got five civilians plus Ben, the four of us, Margery, Camille, Samantha, and Grayson."

"Yeah, that's it. I think more guests were expected,

but with the house in lockdown, they can't get in." Bernard volunteered the information as he dug through Margery's fridge. He emerged triumphant, a local brew in his hand. "Last one. Anyone mind?"

I shook my head, as did Ben. Booze and beer were out—yet another reason to be peeved about the events of the evening. I'd normally feel more sympathy, but not only was I still a little numb from the last murder, I also knew that Isabella was a thoroughly unlikable person. And, for Pete's sake, this was my second real date with Ben.

"Are the pirate duo a couple?" Ben asked.

"Oh, yes," Annalise said with too much glee.

"All right, spill. What's going on with Grayson and Samantha?" I could see she was dying to tell all.

Annalise scooted to the edge of the butcher block and leaned forward. "Samantha's previous fling, the guy before Grayson, turned out to be more than a fling. A huge divergence from her dating MO. She's always been a love-them-and-leave-them kind. But not this last guy. And just as they were looking serious, constantly giving each other goo-goo eyes and being all touchy-feely in public, he goes and gets himself killed. *Mysteriously* killed. There are rumors of a duel. He was big-time traditional, and you know how they feel about injured honor." She paused, blinked, and then added, "But, you know, the details are murky."

I wasn't seeing the juiciness of the story, and there was juice, otherwise Annalise wouldn't be so excited.

Annalise rolled her eyes. "Seriously, Star. You're so out of the loop. She was with a traditional guy who dies, and now she's dating Grayson. Who's totally into her."

I shook my head. Still didn't see it.

"The ex only died about two seconds ago," Annalise said with a smug smile. "You know those old-school witch guys are weird about mourning customs. Do you see Samantha wearing black?"

"Ah." That was all I could say, because people dealt with grief in different ways. Who was I to judge? Maybe Grayson was her rebound guy. Maybe being with him helped her deal with all the sadness of losing her true love. Who knew with a woman like Samantha.

Also, anyone who expected a woman to wear mourning black for eighteen months, in the Texas heat, was a total crackpot with unrealistic expectations.

I didn't grow up in a traditional witch family, but how was that even a thing in this day and age? We were about to enter the twenty-first century, for heaven's sake.

I tried to remind myself that I really shouldn't judge, but I'd already made plenty of judgments about Samantha and her antihuman politics and her nasty attitude. On reflection, I couldn't deny that I was very good at judging.

Eighteen months. All black. In the Texas heat. Witches had some cultural quirks, but that was one of the quirkiest. Especially considering Samantha and what's-his-name hadn't even been engaged.

CeeCee sighed. "It's been more than two seconds since his death. It's been a few months, but everyone has been pretty surprised that she and Grayson have been an item." She arched an eyebrow at me. "If you weren't such an isolationist, you'd know these things."

Ben turned to me with an inquisitive look.

I didn't really want the guy I had a crush on to think I was a weird antisocial freak. Even if I was.

"Yeah, so, ah, Ben and I will go check on the examination of the body." And hopefully get out of there before CeeCee could expound upon my lack of social life amongst the witchy crowd.

CeeCee had a knowing look on her face, one that predicted a future grilling, but she just agreed that was a good idea.

Ben already knew I didn't mingle with non-magical people. I didn't particularly want him piecing together just how much of a loner I was. We could save that for at least the third date.

Just as Ben and I hit the threshold to the living

room, a question I'd meant to ask before came back to me in a flash. "What was the dustup about, the one between Isabella and Grayson?" I asked.

"It was more than a dustup." Annalise's words drew me back into the kitchen.

"What exactly happened?" I asked.

"Fireworks. Enough energy balls to make a light show." CeeCee crossed her arms and tilted her head. "Where were you that you missed the whole thing?"

Ben and I had been on the hunt for a dark and secluded spot. He had a roommate; I lived with my mother. A little alone time of the kissing variety wasn't so untoward around date number two—or so I thought. Especially since we'd been flirting at work for weeks now.

But the universe was strongly disagreeing and shaking its disapproving finger at me.

The first time we'd looked for a quiet spot, apparently at the same time that Grayson and Isabella had been arguing and throwing around magic energy balls, we'd been interrupted by one of the human guests. Mildly awkward. The second time, we'd stumbled on Isabella's corpse. More than awkward.

"You're blushing," Annalise said, her eyes wide.

I frowned at her. "Even if I was, you'd never see it." I might go for a low-key Goth look on a normal day, but today I was all flapper, and that meant lots of powder. I might be a natural blonde under all the black hair dye, but I had the skin of a redhead, freckles included. And a flapper with freckles was hardly authentic. I resisted the urge to touch my face. "The fight? I'm assuming we're not talking duel, just lots of flash and not much magic."

Bernard laughed. "You could say that. Grayson's not really the dueling type. Too old-school for him, and I don't see him having the backbone. That final turn and shoot is unnerving."

I'd never been in a duel, but I understood that it wasn't like the pistols-at-dawn variety. There were rarely seconds, and at the end of the pace-off, the contestants simply turned and fired. It seemed like a game for deranged twelve-year-old boys. Not my style.

"Isabella was upset about something that she claimed Grayson had stolen from her," CeeCee said.

"Yeah, but Grayson said he didn't do it." Annalise's response was suspiciously defensive, and for once this evening, she looked earnest.

Was Annalise using her flirtation with Bernard and me to cover up some actual feelings for Grayson? I sighed. If so, she was useless as a witness.

"Either way," CeeCee said, "he was angry, and he smacked her in the face with an energy ball. It was underhanded, and I doubt it would have landed if he hadn't surprised her."

"He seemed about as surprised as Isabella that it did," Bernard called out from the pantry. He emerged holding a bag of chips. "What? It's true. I think the whole thing was a mistake brought on by short tempers. Isabella is—was—pissed that Grayson cut his mentorship with her short and about the stealing thing, and Grayson was cut up that she was accusing him of theft."

"Oh, man," Ben said. "I don't suppose it was a veil she accused him of stealing?"

"No clue," Bernard replied.

Annalise shrugged.

CeeCee shook her head. "I don't remember, but I'm sure she was still wearing a black veil wrapped around her head and tied to the side, so if that's the one you mean, then no."

Might as well tell them, because it was coming out shortly anyway. "That's the one. It seems to have disappeared."

I got a brief impression that they were surprised, but their reaction was quickly subsumed in a greater display of astonishment when a pitcher smashed to the ground. Red sangria splattered everywhere.

I lifted my hands in exasperation and yelled, "What is with you? Stop it already!"

8

TICK TOCK, OR PROJECTILE VOMITING FORESHADOWED

CeeCee's eyes widened. "It wasn't me."

"Me either." Bernard lifted his hands in surrender.

It took me a second to scan the room for any signs of magic, but again I came up empty. "I know. It's the flipping ghost. He won't stop hassling me."

"Humph. No way," Annalise said. "Margery would have chased the pest away with a cleansing if there were one. And what ghost moves in with a witch? They'd be asking to get bounced out."

"And yet..." I gestured to the sangria that Bernard was now mopping up with a tea towel.

"Telekinesis." Annalise eyed Bernard suspiciously. "It was you, wasn't it?"

Bernard shot her an incredulous look. "Please. I'm a spell guy. Did you hear me muttering any incantations?" He didn't wait for a response, just continued to sop up the mess.

Because he was right: we'd have heard him. That was one of the rules of witch magic. To use a spell, you have to speak it aloud.

Potions had to come in contact with their target—touch, ingestion, inhalation—and spells had to be spoken. There wasn't any getting around that.

Annalise turned to CeeCee, who pointed to her potion. "I'm all about brewing. No telekinesis here." CeeCee looked at me. "Why in the world would Margery not get rid of it? Even if it likes the house enough to return and get bounced out again, she could have done a cleansing right before the party."

Bernard shook out the tea towel in the trash can, the shards of glass tinkling as they fell. He gave the sangria-soaked towel a disgusted look and then chucked it in as well. "Anyone consider that Margery's house is an especially odd choice?" He looked at me expectantly—but I didn't know and shook my head. He said, "All Hallows' Eve, the one night of the year that a ghost can become fully corporeal."

"Ugh, I forgot about the location component." Yet more evidence that my studies were sadly neglected. "A ghost can only become fully corporeal at very specific locations on All Hallows' Eve, and ours is still flitting between the planes."

Bernard pointed a sticky finger at me. "Exactly. What are the locations again?"

"If you two would study more..." CeeCee huffed. "Place of death, home of a loved one, and any physical space with a significant, emotionally charged connection to the ghost. But you're right, Bernard, why specifically the home of a witch? He or she has to know a witch would bounce them out with a cleansing."

"I'll have to ask Margery." Because I had a strong hunch that Margery knew more than she'd said about her unwelcome visitor. I'd bet that she might even know the identity of her resident ghost.

"Good luck with that." Bernard raised his eyebrows at me.

He didn't offer to accompany me. Shocker.

Annalise let out a put-upon sigh. "Should I go with you? It's not like *he's* any kind of backup." She gave Ben a baleful look.

I was a little touched. Annalise was no more a match for Margery than I was. She wouldn't appreciate gushing sentiment, so I just pointed out the obvious. "You have to stay in case the guests need an additional zap. Exactly how bad is that migraine that CeeCee mentioned?"

Annalise tipped her head and squinted. "There's a potential for projectile vomiting, so if you could hurry it up, that would be optimal."

Ben grabbed my hand and pulled me out of the kitchen, calling over his shoulder, "Send us a five-minute warning."

Once we were clear of the kitchen and approaching the stairs, he said, "She won't do anything to you, right? I mean, when you ask why she's been withholding information about the ghost. She has to know who it is."

I considered equivocation, but landed on honesty. He needed to know the score, especially if we were going to be dating. And if a second Society murder didn't chase him off, then he might just be in for the long haul.

"I don't *think* so, but she can be fussy about questioning her authority, so it's certainly possible she'll take a short-tempered shot at me." In a hopeful tone, I added, "Camille's there."

Ben made an adorably protective growly noise.

I'd reassure him more fully, but I didn't want to fib. And Ben knew all about Camille's strengths and weaknesses. Alex, my ex, had been quite vocal during the last murder investigation. He didn't value her strengths as much as he should, and he wouldn't listen—really listen—to my reasoning for keeping her as my mentor. There was a reason he was my *ex*.

But Ben knew how much trust I placed in Camille.

I eyed the staircase with some trepidation.

Ben gestured for me to precede him up the stairs.

When I hesitated, he touched my back. "I'll be right behind you. Until we figure out why this ghost becomes intermittently hysterical, I'm sticking close."

Ben might not have any magic, but he was solid. Solid reliable, solid big. Just solid. It made me feel better having him at my back. Which didn't mean I wasn't hanging on to the stair railing with a death grip.

Since I was inching up the stairs, I had time to consider the suspect list. "The mysterious ghost is looking less likely. It would be difficult for a ghost that wasn't fully corporeal to drown a witch."

"A powerful witch, from what everyone's been saying. And why isn't anyone wet? Wouldn't whoever drowned her be soaked?"

Clinging to the rail, I looked over my shoulder. "Drying clothes is simple magic. Kitchen magic, they call it. So I wouldn't expect damp clothes. Honestly, if the killer used something like Annalise's knockout spell, they might not have even gotten wet."

"Everyone seems pretty impressed that she can do it. Do you think someone has the same spell?"

My grip loosened as I considered whether someone else had that particular spell up their sleeve. Witches could be very proprietary, especially if a particular working of magic had commercial potential. "Possibly. Developed in parallel, stolen—yeah, it could be." I tightened my grip and continued upward.

"You're amazing at this," Ben said.

"What?"

"Fitting into a world I know is strange to you, learning about magic, keeping calm in the middle of a murder, investigating—"

"Okay, already." But I was grinning. It was nice to be admired. I looked over my shoulder. "If I wasn't clinging to the banister for dear life and in the middle of a murder investigation, I would kiss you." I caught his grin before I turned my attention back to climbing the stairs and arriving in one piece.

"Speaking of our investigation, I've got a few questions. Grayson's argument for one, Margery's knowledge of the ghost, and the veil—something's hinky with that veil."

"How do you mean?" I asked.

"I don't think Grayson stole it, because CeeCee said Isabella had the scarf wrapped around her hair during the fight."

"Good point," I said. "I guess the fact that Grayson was the one to point out it was missing was a clue that it wasn't him, too."

"What about Samantha?"

"No motive." I climbed the last few steps and

made a beeline for the first bedroom door—away from the stairs.

"And all of that stuff with her dating history?" Ben asked. "It was odd, right? And in a murder investigation, anything odd is noteworthy."

"Yes."

We were standing in front of a spare bedroom—an empty bedroom—and if we weren't on the clock—

"We've got about a half hour."

And the man was a mind reader on top of all his other talents. Not that I was seriously considering it, what with the deadline...and the murder and all.

I pivoted toward the master bedroom.

"What about Camille?" Ben asked.

"What about Camille?" Then I realized he meant as the possible murderer and decided he wasn't such a great mind reader after all. "She's not on the suspect list."

"Okay..."

"No. Just no." I stopped. "The kitchen and the master bedroom are at completely opposite ends of the house, and it's a big house."

Ben nodded. "Four, five thousand square feet. A bit much for one person, I'd think, but to each their own."

"Right, but my point is that the center of casual parties is the kitchen."

"Or the patio."

"Come on. It's Texas, and even in October it's a gazillion degrees outside." I caught the expression on his face and said, "Okay, the patio is the center of a barbecue. Cocktails, it's the formal living room. Holiday meals, the dining room. But for beer, queso, and taquitos—"

"The kitchen." He frowned. "This is definitely a beer and taquitos type of do. And you're right, most of us were in the kitchen or the second living area right next to it."

"Which is why you and I snuck up here for—you know—only to be rudely interrupted by a corpse. So, how did everyone else find us so quickly? Before we'd raised any alarm?"

Ben tipped his head toward the master bedroom. "That sounds like it might actually be important. Let's go find out."

9

MARGERY'S PLUMBING COMES UNDER SUSPICION

I popped the question without ceremony as soon I opened the bathroom door. "How did so many people so quickly end up in an isolated area of the house just seconds after Ben and I discovered Isabella?"

Camille raised her hand. "It was me. I escorted the doctor—CeeCee's friend, I believe—to this bathroom. The half bath near the kitchen was occupied with someone waiting, and the other downstairs bathroom was having some kind of plumbing problem."

With Camille's revelation—Margery's plumbing was defective—you'd have thought Camille had made a personal attack on Margery. She lifted her chin and said, "Excuse me? There is absolutely nothing wrong with my plumbing."

"Regardless of what you may or may not believe, the toilet wasn't flushing. I'm surprised no one told you, since it looks like it might have overflowed."

Margery's eyes bugged out. "If there's water damage—"

"We've got a murder, Margery. Focus. And besides, someone mopped up the mess. There's no water damage." Camille looked a lot less annoyed by the outburst than I was. The woman had infinite patience.

"My towels? Those towels—" Margery grunted as Camille elbowed her. "Ah, yes, the towels are, of course, replaceable."

I took a moment to recall the glimpse of grief I'd seen on Margery's face when she'd first spotted Isabella's body. I needed the reminder that she wasn't a monster, because I was feeling some pretty intense dislike for her right now.

Time to borrow Camille's words: *we've got a murder; focus.*

"So you don't usually have plumbing problems?" I asked, because I had a sneaking suspicion I knew what might be clogging up those pipes.

"Of course not," Margery replied, then her gaze narrowed.

"Ben, do you think you can have a look at the downstairs bathroom? The one on this side of the house, not the half bath near the kitchen."

"Got it," he replied with a grim look.

"Bennett, one moment." How Margery knew Ben's full name was anyone's guess, but that she used it was interesting. Margery was a fan of full names...and maybe was a fan of Ben's? "The cleaning cupboard is under the front stairs. I'm sure you'll find a plunger there."

Ben headed off to plunge a toilet—and hopefully find a veil. He really was a trouper.

I turned to Grayson. "So, the argument you had with Isabella this evening?"

A look of chagrin passed over his face. "It was a misunderstanding—in part. You know, she wasn't the amazing mentor everyone said."

Witches didn't have an issue with speaking ill of the dead. I heard all sorts of nasty things about the deceased. Not usually on the day they were murdered, but it wasn't particularly surprising.

When Margery didn't jump in—she was distracted, intermittently eyeing the door and then scanning the room—I said, "So your argument was over your mentorship?"

"In part. I left because she wasn't fulfilling her promises." He hesitated.

"And?"

"And..." He tipped his head to the left, clearly contemplating what to say. "I might have taken some of our ongoing projects when I left."

That caught Margery's attention, because she chuckled. "Serves the old bat right. She always was too tight-fisted with her mentees."

My eyes widened, then I tried to mask my surprise. Too late; I'd been seen.

With a fond look in her eye, Margery said, "Don't judge. Her possessiveness was one of her endearing qualities. I'm just not surprised that it caused her problems."

Being a witch and being raised in the witching community were two very different experiences. I didn't think like them, and I wasn't sure I wanted to. I swallowed a sigh, then turned to Grayson. "And that was all you were arguing over, some stolen potions?"

"And spells." He arched an eyebrow. "Some really good spells. But I already have them, and she wasn't getting them back from me, so there was no reason to kill her over them."

Maybe I shouldn't have, but I believed him. Which meant Margery was next on the list. Whatever was going on with her was all tied up with the ghost. And the ghost was tied up with the veil, and the veil was missing.

If I wasn't on a tight deadline... I gritted my teeth and went for it. "Margery, why—"

"Why am I being haunted?" Margery gave me a baleful look. "That's what you want to know, isn't it?"

"Quit it with the evil eye, will you?" Camille said.

"It's not her fault you've been acting suspiciously. I think everyone will agree, your behavior has been odd, and we have had a murder."

Grayson kept his mouth shut, but Samantha nodded with a mean look in her eye. She must have been feeling especially brave, because picking a fight with Margery wasn't great for a person's health.

"You know who it is, don't you?" I asked.

Margery folded her hands together. "I have my suspicions, but I couldn't be sure. Can't be sure now, because the veil is gone."

At which point Ben proved once again how exceptional he was. He walked in with a plastic bag in his hand. He lifted the bag and said, "I've got it."

Everyone in the room turned to look at him.

"Ah, I think this is it. A black lace veil, about so long." He indicated a distance of about three feet. Everyone continued to stare. "I did wash it first."

But the silence was nothing to do with the previous whereabouts of the veil. Not even remotely.

Margery looked relieved.

Camille pleasantly surprised.

Grayson... Grayson looked wary, then worried. He backed away from Samantha with a look of trepidation.

And Samantha, Samantha looked...guilty.

10

WHO DONE DID IT

"You were in that bathroom," Grayson said, "only a few minutes before the body was found."

Samantha shrugged. "So what? I'm sure someone used it after me."

"Was there anyone waiting to use the bathroom?" I asked Grayson. Not a question that I'd trust Samantha to answer with honesty at this point.

His gaze riveted on Samantha, he said, "No. No one. And then a few minutes later, we heard a scream. Just enough time for the next person who tried to use the bathroom to make their way up to the master bath and see the corpse."

"You can't know that," Samantha said, but she was inching toward the door.

Cornered animals were much more likely to

attack, and I didn't want to get zapped by an unexpected energy ball, so I kept a close eye on her while I tried to tug a resistant Ben behind me.

"No, we can't know that," I agreed. "But it's the truth, isn't it?"

As Samantha slowly moved to the door, I shifted so that Ben was behind me. He was a foot taller than me, but I was pretty sure I could concoct a shield that covered both of us. I'd done it before.

Then I remembered that we'd been touching last time. I reached behind me for his hand and put it on my hip. And that was when I realized who the ghost was. Who he had to be. It was Samantha's ex. The man she'd been head over heels in love with, who'd mysteriously died. He was the ghost.

Now if I could just get the whole story out of Samantha, preferably confession-style, and, even more importantly, before Margery zapped her into the next plane of existence, then things would be looking up.

She was almost to the door—I couldn't believe Margery hadn't made a move. I glanced at Margery to find her preoccupied with a pair of nail scissors that danced menacingly in the air. Margery was being distracted by the resident ghost.

I blurted out the first thing that came to my mind. "You wanted to see your lover again."

It worked, because Samantha stopped about a foot from the door.

And then I heard the sound of the nail scissors as they hit the tile floor, followed by the reverberating thud as the bathroom door slammed shut.

Oh, no. Margery—

A dazzling green ball of energy whooshed by my ear and would have hit Samantha directly in the chest but for a hastily erected shield.

"Margery!" I hollered.

But she ignored me and let loose a second dense ball of green magic.

"Stop. Now." Camille didn't raise her voice, but there was a terrible quality to it that I'd not heard before.

"You okay?" Ben whispered in my ear.

I nodded. I hadn't been singed—but Camille's odd tone was giving me goose bumps. She looked—sounded—scarier than Samantha, our outed murderer.

Camille's voice lightened, and when she spoke it was with a cool, dispassionate look on her face. "If you want to get rid of your ghost, maybe it's time you just stop and listen, Margery." With just a hint of the earlier menace in her voice, Camille added, "Unless you want to be haunted forever?"

Margery didn't respond, but she also didn't chuck another sizzling magic ball.

Amidst the distraction, Samantha had crept closer to the exit. The rattle of the knob being jiggled brought our attention back to her.

The ghost had prevented Margery from flinging magic willy-nilly, but now it had turned its attention to Samantha. Our ghost wasn't letting her go.

My patience was gone. Five minutes ago, gone. "Who's the ghost?" I said.

Ben lifted the bag he still held clenched in his hand. "You might as well tell us, because we can look ourselves."

"Excellent point. I'll take that." Though I had no desire to chat with someone beyond the grave, it was worth the gamble. I hoped a nudge would be enough to get one of the two witches who had a clue talking.

Ben handed me the bag, and I got a nasty shock. A witch didn't have to *look through* the veil to see ghosts. Touching—even through a plastic bag—was enough.

A dead man in a tux held the door firmly shut. He wasn't transparent in the sense that I could see through him, but I knew he wasn't fully on this plane. My witch sight at work?

Concentrating, I focused tightly on the man, eliminating my peripheral vision, and then a shimmer appeared around the edges of his body. *That* was my witch sight.

I closed my eyes. The sparkle was giving me a headache. When I opened them, he was still there—without the sparkles—but I could see now why he'd looked otherworldly. Everything about him was washed out. All the colors were present, just faded, and only a little. As I focused in on him, I'd swear the colors brightened.

"You see him, don't you?" Samantha asked.

Since she was sitting hunched against the door and the man in the tux was still holding fast to the knob, they overlapped each other in a way that made my head spin. How had that not been my first clue?

"He didn't love me, not like I loved him." She rattled the locked door handle. "He never did." She rattled the handle again, and when she found it still locked, she leaned against the door and slowly slid to the ground.

"I did love her. Clearly more than she did me." The ghost's eyes darted to Grayson, but he quickly looked away, an expression of disgust on his face.

My earlier argument about people grieving in different ways didn't seem persuasive in this situation, but I had to say something. "That's not exactly—"

"What? Fair?" the ghost said with a pained expression. "We were engaged. Did she tell you that?"

"No, ah— What's your name?"

"Nathaniel." There was a mulish cast to his face that reminded me too much of a young, petulant boy.

Not, I suspected, a good sign. "All right, Nathaniel. No, I didn't know that you were engaged."

Samantha inhaled sharply. "Nothing matters now. I just wanted to know how you died, so I could move on, but you won't even give me that. All because of some stupid old mourning ritual."

Oh, no. Here came the drama. For such a mercenary lot, witches really could be ridiculous drama queens.

I considered my options. The bag could fall to the ground "accidentally." I could chuck it at Camille, so she had to witness the unfolding melodrama. Or I could just burn the thing. It wasn't that damp. Anything to get me away from the soap opera that was unfolding.

Ben leaned down and whispered, "Ten minutes."

Exasperation welled up, and not far behind was the projectile-vomiting image Annalise had firmly planted in my head.

I lifted my hands. "All right, people. We've got a dead woman, so start explaining. Samantha, why did you need to kill Isabella to get a look through the veil? How did you even know she'd have it tonight?"

Samantha looked surprised. "I didn't know she

had it, or that it would be here tonight. I was completely surprised." She shot a nasty look at Margery. "Ask *her* why I had to kill Isabella."

Margery was fuming. "You didn't have to kill her. I'm surprised you were even capable."

"You know Annalise and I were roommates? She hadn't quite perfected that little knockout gag, but she was close. I just took it, tweaked it, and saved it for a rainy day." Samantha smirked. "Today it was just pouring. Uh, metaphorically."

This time I didn't even try to hide the sigh. "We got that. We're on a bit of a deadline here, so— Samantha, why did you kill Isabella?"

She bit her lip. "Yeah. That was an accident."

Every person in the room turned to look at her with varying degrees of incredulity plastered across their faces.

Funny enough, it was Ben, the single non-magical occupant of the room, who spoke. "She passed out sprawled across the lip of the tub, and then you took the headscarf." With a flash of sympathy in his eyes, he said. "You didn't consider that she might slump down, slipping face-first into the water."

Margery inhaled sharply. It was either she or Camille—from her reaction, likely Margery herself —who had filled the tub with water and set pretty lit candles afloat in it, never once considering the bizarre turn of events that would unfold that evening, or the pivotal role that water would play.

Samantha was shaking her head. "I didn't. Really, I didn't. She just wouldn't let me use it, and I just wanted..."

We knew what she wanted: to see her lost love again.

"Wait, did you know that Nathaniel was haunting Margery's house?"

Samantha shook her head.

Nathaniel, silently observing till now, spoke. "I was in the room when Samantha took the veil. She saw me immediately."

Margery narrowed her eyes suspiciously at Samantha. "You didn't know he was here?"

Samantha shook her head again, and a tear slipped down her face.

Nathaniel pointed a finger at Margery. "You didn't deserve Isabella." A frustrated look passed over his face when he realized I was the only one who could see him. He turned to me and said, "Isabella wouldn't let Samantha have access to the veil, because she knew by then that I was the ghost haunting Margery—and that Margery had killed me."

"Whoa... What? Margery? Wait, what?" Too many murders, that was what my brain was telling me.

11

MURDER MATH

"What did he say?" Margery snapped.

Samantha turned to Margery. "It was you? You killed him? You killed him!" Her voice grew shriller with each word until she was screeching.

Never, ever again was I attending a witch party.

I might be a witch, but these were not my people.

First there'd been a murder, but actually not—more of a manslaughter? I was hazy on the law, and since it wouldn't be applied in this case anyway, it didn't really matter. So we went from murder, to almost murder, to a murder accusation. The math was mind-boggling when I considered it was *murder* I was adding and subtracting.

I drew a breath, intending and failing to calm myself, then clapped my hands loudly.

Once I had everyone's attention, I started to tick off the facts on my fingers. "Margery, the ghost says you killed him. I'd say he's our best source for his own death. Nathaniel, you're a lunatic who's been trying to kill me all night, so I'm not so sure I'm sad she did it. Samantha, you're responsible for Isabella's death, but not intentionally, more through..." I searched for the right word. "Incompetence? And I'm sure the Society will consider that."

I took a step back and a deep breath.

Nathaniel followed me with a raised finger. "I was not trying to kill you. Do you know how difficult it is to communicate from the other side?"

"You tried to push me down the stairs." I didn't even try to keep the exasperation from my voice. To Ben I said, "He's claiming no murderous intent. He was *trying to communicate*. Please."

Samantha and Margery were glaring daggers at each other, and I realized we still hadn't quite sorted out the murder-duel question.

I was a little done with Nathaniel and his "communicating," so I turned to Margery and said, "Any chance you'd like to clarify how Nathaniel died?"

She rose to her full height. "It was a duel."

Which was completely legal...if shady as heck ethically and in direct defiance of Margery's own very publicly stated opposition to dueling.

"No, no it wasn't." Nathaniel was so livid that I

could clearly see the red in his cheeks, even as washed out as he was.

I was getting the petulant-boy vibe from him again. I really, really didn't get what Samantha had seen in this tool.

"He says it wasn't." I turned to him and asked, "How was it not a duel? You agreed to duel?" He nodded curtly. "You started at ten paces?" Again, he nodded. I shrugged. "Where's the issue?" Other than the complete idiocy of actually dueling, but I kept that to myself.

Samantha jumped to her feet when I started to ask questions about dueling.

"She fired early," Nathaniel said.

Which I repeated.

"No," Margery bellowed. "I did not! On one, I fired on one." Which was, in fact, how one dueled in the witching world.

"But we're supposed to fire *after* one." Nathaniel crossed his arms with a stubborn look on his face. And this was the same guy who wanted his fiancée to wear black for eighteen months because it was "tradition," and yet he didn't know the basic rules of one of the oldest (and most idiotic) forms of conflict resolution in the witching world.

"You're a complete and utter nincompoop. Learn the rules, you idiot!" At which point I dropped the bag with the wet veil. "Camille, banish this nitwit. Please."

A strangled noise emerged from the back of her throat and her lips were pulled tight. Once she'd gotten a handle on the monstrous laugh she was holding back, she uttered a brief but effective cleansing spell. "Begone, unwanted visitor. Leave this house forthwith." A little crackle started with the word "begone" and a pop followed "forthwith."

"Wait!" Samantha called, but she was too late.

Camille rubbed the ash from her fingers; not that anyone had noticed her dropping a pinch of it—or the salt or the sage—earlier. The rest of her ingredients were proprietary, so I could only guess. And since the potion was intended for the house—the *house*, after all, was haunted, not Margery herself—dusting the floor of the bathroom with the ingredient had been sufficient.

Most witches needed a prepared potion to cleanse a house of a ghost, so I was sure Camille's swift and apparently spell-driven cleansing shocked everyone. What they didn't know was that Camille, my much maligned and undervalued mentor, was always prepared.

I'd taken a step back, bumping into Ben, when I saw Samantha's face.

Her face contorted with rage. "He's gone, you, you...you hag!"

She chucked a nasty, misshapen blob of dark purple magic at me. Someone was letting their emotions mess with their magic.

Her sad attack was easily deflected—by Camille. I had a shield in place, but deflection was a little out of my league. The ugly, not-quite-ball-shaped thing sizzled against the bathroom wall, leaving a scorch mark.

Fortifying my shield and making sure that Ben was still in physical contact with me, I eyed the room. Whose side everyone was going to be on if this devolved into a magic-flinging mess was the question of the moment.

But then Samantha did the unexpected.

She bawled.

12

THE COMMENCEMENT OF ONE VERY INTERRUPTED DATE

Big, fat, angry tears rolled down Samantha's face. She wasn't a pretty crier. There was snot and smeared mascara and lots of hiccupping. "I lo—ove—ed him."

She was barely coherent, what with all the gasping and sobbing.

Ben pulled a packet of tissues out of his pocket. Leave it to the funeral director to have tissues on hand in a crisis. Then again, toilet paper would have done in a pinch. We were still in the bathroom.

I passed the tissues along to her. "It's not like he's gone forever." I stopped myself from saying anything else. This woman—upset though she may be—had killed another woman through her negligence, and her actions had been fueled by the same deranged love that spurred her tears.

She blew her nose, and then said, much more clearly, "He won't come back. He's so mad." She blinked. "And you embarrassed him."

The truth hurt—at least it did when you were a nincompoop like Nathaniel. Samantha was not an idiot. Yes, she'd killed a woman, but that had been self-absorption and a lack of care for others more than actual stupidity. So why did a not-entirely-stupid woman fall for someone like Nathaniel?

"If it makes you feel any better," I said, "it seems like his death was an honest mistake. He flubbed the dueling rules. He even admitted it. He miscounted. No murder or misdeeds involved."

But that only got the sobbing started again. Which, now that I thought about it, made sense. She had said that I'd embarrassed him and that was part of why she didn't expect him to return.

I was terrible at comforting people. Good thing I was working the back of the shop at the funeral home.

The worst part of the thing was that dueling usually wasn't lethal. Deflection, shielding, both worked well...if one counted appropriately and was prepared.

I extricated myself before I said that, or something even more idiotic, out loud.

As Samantha noisily cried, I discreetly, quietly

asked the others, "Everyone okay with Alex cleaning up the rest of the mess?"

The Society was keen on hanging—which made me cringe—but they weren't too terribly bothered with murder...unless there was a "reveal" risk and magic was about to become front page news or someone important, someone with influence that extended beyond death, had been killed.

Unfortunately for Samantha, Isabella had been a woman with influential friends, and Cornelius was trying to make a go of a more just judicial review. On the other hand, it hadn't exactly been murder. No intent, no murder—basically.

I sighed. Who knew where this one would end? I liked to think there'd be some kind of punishment for Samantha, but something appropriate to the crime—not hanging, contrary to the Society's predilections.

Margery was likely to have significant sway in Samantha's sentencing. Maybe if I had a word with Alex, perhaps explained about the dueling and maybe that we'd keep quiet about it...if Margery wouldn't pursue hanging.

No one was jumping up and down demanding I keep Alex out of witch business, so I asked for a phone.

Grayson retrieved a clamshell mobile he'd

tucked into the side of his pirate boot and handed it to me.

"You can push a call through, can't you, Margery?" I asked, waving the small phone in the air.

With a curt nod, Margery snapped her fingers.

I punched in Alex's number and was glad Ben wasn't paying close enough attention to see that I still had my ex's number memorized.

It rang once before Alex picked up. I didn't wait for a greeting, just said, "I have an urgent pickup for you at Margery's house. You better hurry." I paused. "It's complicated."

Alex groaned, then said, "On my way."

Thank goodness for small favors. Alex was good at his job and took it seriously, whatever his failings as a boyfriend. I returned Grayson's phone, trying not to dwell on his situation. Except for Isabella, he'd probably had the worst evening. Samantha was supposed to be his girlfriend, and she'd been carrying such a flaming torch for her ex that she'd committed almost murder/manslaughter. Man, I needed to look that up.

Or not.

I returned to Ben's side with a relieved smile.

"It's all handled, then?" Ben asked.

"I think so." I gave him an apologetic look. "I'm sorry the evening's been ruined."

He glanced at his watch. "It hasn't yet, but we're well past your friend Annalise's deadline, and if we're here when the other guests wake up, it might be."

I stretched up on my tiptoes and kissed him.

When I shot Camille a pleading look, she smiled back at me. "Margery and I will handle Alex."

And with that blessing, I grabbed Ben's hand and tugged him behind me as I practically ran out of the room.

Ben followed obligingly behind until we got to the stairs, then he slowed down and stopped. "How, in the midst of more experienced witches, did you end up leading the investigation?"

"Easy. Camille probably saw it as a learning opportunity. Like I've said before—"

"I know, she's often underestimated."

"Exactly right. I'd guess that Margery was trying to keep a low profile because she had a very good idea of who was haunting her house and why. And I know that she wouldn't want the fact that she'd been dueling to get out, especially since the duel went awry. More pessimistic souls might believe she'd cheated to win."

"But not you."

"No, never me. Just call me the epitome of optimism."

Ben grinned. "You can be as sarcastic as you like —I know that underneath a layer or twelve beats the heart of a true optimist."

I laughed. "Really? Just keep telling yourself that."

Ben eyed the guest room that I'd considered sneaking into earlier. "What were we doing before we stumbled onto a murder investigation?"

"Ha—I do believe I remember." I kissed his chin, which was all I could reach with his head tilted away from me. "And I'd love to continue—but we're getting out of this house first."

"Sold." He leaned down and kissed me. After several very satisfying seconds—minutes?—he said, "We better head out now, before the projectile vomiting starts and your ex shows up at the front door. *That* might ruin the mood."

Apparently, for my funeral home director date, dead bodies and murder investigations were no detriment to a good time. I adored that about Ben.

I chuckled. I was practically giddy, and that wasn't usually me. Only Ben could make me giddy. "You know? I think you have this dating-a-witch thing down."

STAR AND BEN continue their sleuthing adventures in *Tickle the Dragon's Tail*. They have to help a dragon who's been falsely accused of frying a vampire. Marge is no murderer, and our sleuthing duo make it their mission to prove her innocent. Turn the page to read more...

TICKLE THE DRAGON'S TAIL EXCERPT
CHAPTER ONE

Getting my own apartment meant that I no longer had to live with my mother. Good thing, since she still didn't have a clue that magic was real or that her daughter practiced witchcraft. Mom's ignorance had proven awkward and inconvenient on more than a few occasions.

Moving into my new digs meant that my back was aching from shifting my thrift-store finds up two flights of stairs to my freshly painted—but decidedly chintzy—place. A girl on a budget had to settle for some chintz if she wanted her own place. And thrift-store shopping. No new furniture for me in the foreseeable future.

Witches might make the big bucks, but I was technically still a witch in training...and a grad student who hadn't finished her thesis, a part-time employee at my mentor's crystal shop, and a part-time makeup artist and girl Friday at my boyfriend's funeral home. A little hustle was helping to pay the bills while I finished my studies, both magical and academic.

Hustle also helped when it came to practicing witchcraft in an apartment complex filled with people. *Bunches* of people, none of whom had any inkling that magic existed. Hiding my witchy talents from nosy neighbors had just become that much harder.

I might be able to talk my way out of some flashy magic exposure, but it was best to keep the bangs, flares, and sparkles to a minimum and save myself the trouble.

"Star," Ben called out from the small balcony. He'd offered to set up my plants, and since they were heavy as heck, I'd agreed. Men were good for that sort of thing.

"Just a second. I'm almost done unpacking this box." The box containing my meager kitchen supplies, which would allow us to cook up some of the food we both were in desperate need of after hauling furniture all day.

"Yeah, hon, you're gonna want to see this. Now."

Uh-oh. Ben wasn't *that* guy. You know the one: bossy, rude, demanding. His tone meant trouble was afoot.

As I jogged the few steps from my miniscule kitchen to my balcony, I knew in my bones it was magic melodrama. I'd been working on giving Ben a view into my world—literally, using a combination of spells and charms—so now he could see some magic that other mundanes couldn't.

Also, if there was going to be a kink on moving day, it would be magical. Magic was fickle like that, picking the worst moments to go askew. At least, that was how it felt to *me*. My mentor Camille assured me it was all in my head.

I stumbled to a halt in front of the sliding glass doors.

All I saw was Ben pressed back against the glass. My red-headed hunk's tush might have temporarily distracted me, otherwise I might have noticed the absolute stillness of his body more quickly. But once I did, it didn't take long for me to get a better read on the situation. I looked past him to find a visitor on my balcony.

The balcony door was cracked just wide enough for me to slip through. I darted outside and practically squealed, "Marge!"

Maybe I sounded like a twelve-year-old getting her first pony. Not shocking. It wasn't every day that a dragon came to visit.

She lifted her chin from my balcony, gave me

what I could only guess was intended to be a grin, then fluttered her long lashes at Ben.

"Uh…" Ben inched closer to me and whispered, "Do you see that? The scales and the teeth." He cleared his throat. "And what's with the eyelashes? Is she *flirting* with me?"

Marge tilted her head coyly, which I took to mean, "Yes, I'm flirting with you, you hot hunk of man."

I wrapped an arm around Ben's waist. "Yes, I see her. Her name is Marge, and she's definitely flirting with you. Aren't you, Marge?"

Her lashes fluttered madly.

"She…" Ben quickly turned his attention from me to Marge. "Sorry. You understand us." Then he shook his head. "Of course you do. Marge, please tell me the neighbors can't see you. Star just moved in today, and it would be great if we could keep her here. Her previous living situation wasn't the best."

My mom wasn't *that* bad. But then I tried to imagine what Mom would do if she found a dragon on her doorstep. Her reaction would be wildly different from Ben's calm acceptance.

My guy was the best.

Something niggled, something about Marge and my mom… A long forgotten memory surfaced: my mom almost *had* found a dragon on her doorstep. I met Marge when I was sixteen. She'd turned up on the curb in front of my mom's house. She'd given me an anxiety attack, because I'd been sure I was about to be outed to my mother, but Marge had acted so much like a sad, overgrown Labrador that I'd been completely enchanted by her.

Actually, she was acting in a very similar fashion now.

Marge gave Ben and me a sad puppy-dog look.

But that sweetly mournful look didn't answer Ben's question.

"No one can see you, can they?" I cringed at the hopeful note in my voice. I didn't have much experience with the kinds of spells that hid large moving objects, so I hadn't a clue if one was attached to her right now.

Marge's eyes rolled up and to the left, and she looked about as sheepish as a dragon could look.

"I really hope that's uncertainty and not guilt," Ben whispered. "Because if she's visible and anyone can see her—"

"Yep. Big problem." I pointed at Marge. "Stay." Then I backed into the apartment, dragging Ben with me.

"Is she really three stories tall?" Ben asked as I pulled him into the kitchen.

"Uh, what? No. Maybe. I don't know. She has a really long neck. But, Ben, what the heck? There's a dragon on my balcony!"

"Isn't that my line?" He reached behind me for something on the counter. "Boyfriend freaks out and melts down when confronted by scaly monster with giant fangs. It sounds like a part I'm well qualified to play. One that's more appropriate for the person in the room without magic." He kissed my cheek and pressed my cordless phone into my hand.

Blinking at it, I shook my head.

"Camille?" he said gently. "Your mentor?"

"Oh! Right. Of course." I dialed her number from memory. I'd have come to that conclusion on my own...eventually. I was allowed a moment to collect myself when a mythical creature showed up on my doorstep. That was an official Big Life Event, not lessened one iota by the fact that the mythical creature was named Marge.

Camille's familiar voice filled my ear. "Camille's Crystals. How can I best brighten your day?"

"It's me." I licked my lips. "Marge is back."

A noise that sounded a lot like "eeep" chirped in my ear. My mentor was capable, powerful, and prepared for all eventualities. She also wasn't the squeaking type.

"Camille? What's wrong?"

"Uh, Marge is in a lot of trouble right now. Star, she can't be there."

Marge was tied up with some important memories. The passage of time might have buried them, but once jogged loose, I couldn't help but remember how important that day had been to me. Not only did my not-quite-adult self meet a dragon—a real-life, eyelash-fluttering, steam-breathing, purply-blue and green dragon—but Marge had also been the catalyst that had pushed me to accept the concrete reality of magic.

Heck, if a dragon showing up on your doorstep doesn't convince you that magic is real, I'm not sure what would.

I quickly considered my options. "Let's say she's not here. Let's say it was a drunk tequila moment. I'm completely plastered. You know, moving is really stressful and it makes a lady want to drink."

"Uh-huh."

"Right." I bit my lip and my gaze slipped to meet Ben's. "So, having not seen Marge, maybe you could tell me what kind of trouble she's in?"

In an emotionless tone, she said, "She's been accused of frying Alistair."

My heart thumped erratically in my chest. "Riii-ight. Gotta run. Bye, Camille." As soon as I ended the call, I made a beeline for the box with the booze.

"Tequila? Is now really the time?" Ben asked. Poor, innocent, uninformed Ben.

"Yep. No question about it, and you'll want one, too."

Because there was a Marge manhunt underway

and probably a horde of vampires hot on her trail. The trail that led to our balcony.

After I downed one shot, I poured another and clinked with Ben's. "Marge has been accused of toasting a very influential vamp in the area."

"Toasted?"

"Toasted. Fried. Like a squishy marshmallow."

Ben knew me. He knew I wouldn't let the masses, vampiric or otherwise, get their murdering hands on my dragon friend.

"Right." That was all he said. No complaining, no "what if she did it," no hasty retreat out of my apartment or my life. "That's all right. We'll sort it out."

We. Which meant him and me, together.

Best. Guy. Ever.

But he did toss back that tequila shot and another one for good luck.

To read Star and Ben's fiery, dragon-filled adventure, download your copy of *Tickle the Dragon's Tail* now!

ABOUT THE AUTHOR

When Cate's not tapping away at her keyboard or in deep contemplation of her next fanciful writing project, she's sweeping up hairy dust bunnies and watching British mysteries.

Cate is from Austin, Texas (where many of her stories take place) but has recently migrated north to Boise, Idaho, where soup season (her favorite time of year) lasts more than two weeks.

She's worked as an attorney, a dog trainer, and in various other positions, but writer is the hands-down winner. She's thankful readers keep reading, so she can keep writing!

For bonus materials and updates, visit her website to join her mailing list: www.CateLawley.com.